Alan Blackwood

Pot Shots

novum pro

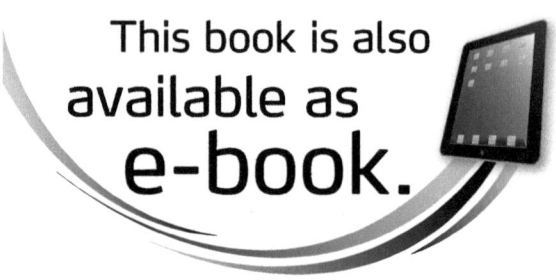

www.novum-publishing.co.uk

All rights of distribution, including film, radio, television, photomechanical reproduction, sound carrier, electronic media and reprint in extracts, are reserved. Printed in the European Union, using environmentally-friendly, chlorine-free and acid-free paper.	© 2016 novum publishing ISBN 978-3-99048-214-8 Editor: Nicola Ratcliff Cover picture: Clare Johnson Cover design, layout & typesetting: novum publishing **www.novum-publishing.co.uk**

TWO'S COMPANY

'May I?' She slipped into the seat across the table with a little silken kiss of her legs. She smiled and raised her glass, rattling her bangles. 'Cheers!'

The ship began to roll with the open sea. 'I love going places,' she said. 'Don't you?'

I topped up my own glass and shook my head. 'Not at night. Water and darkness, I feel lost, like crossing the river Lethe.'

The mascara, the eyelashes, gave her the wide-eyed gaze of a doll. 'Are you a writer, or something?'

Nice of her to ask. 'Sort of. I've had a few things published. Nothing special.'

'It must be wonderful to write.' She watched the lights of the ferry going the other way. 'Ships that pass in the night,' she added dreamily.

So why was she drinking with a stranger, on this ship, in the middle of the night?

A distant beam of light swung in a lazy arc. The French coast. 'Hasn't the time gone quickly!' She smiled again, over my shoulder. 'All right, darling?' Bill had to take his pill and go and lie down as soon as they got on board.

I saw them again, down on the car deck, with two stickers, Bill and Sandra, across the top of their windscreen. Then we were off, in a cloud of exhaust.

Ships that pass in the night. And hangovers that don't.

CAT FLAP

The more you wait for the phone to ring, the more it won't. It was the front door entry phone that made me jump. A woman asked if she could leave a notice at our block of flats about a missing cat.

Two of them waited downstairs by the door, wrapped up against the bitter east wind beneath a sky as grey and hard as pumice, while the face of a bright young tabby stared back at me from their sad notice. Her name was Biscuit.

'Poor little Biscuit,' I said, but they'd already gone, too cold and too eaten up with anxiety to hang about.

At least it got a bit warmer in the next few days, with billowing white clouds, and rain to trickle down all those other notices, stuck on fences and round lamp-posts, of the same furry little face.

'Any luck?' I was sure it was one of those women, now in plastic mac and calf-length green wellies. 'Biscuit,' I reminded her. She frowned and hurried on down the street.

It was worth a shot, for someone who had a thing about calf-length green wellies and two ladies who might be more than just good friends.

I switched on the kettle, dropped a tea bag in a mug, and tried not to wait for anything.

DOG DAYS

They call it 'la canicule' in those parts, meaning little dog, a heat wave that comes with the appearance in the night sky of Cirius, or the Dog Star. The Dog Days, in other words, when you can almost weigh the heat, and if you're a dog you just lie around and pant and scratch your fleas.

Except for the grumpy pug-nosed Pekinese under the table next to ours in the restaurant. With a fancy blue ribbon tied round his neck, he just whined and whimpered and yapped.

Nor, I think, was it the heat. It was another dog, nearly the size of a mule and with a coat as thick as a Persian rug, flopped out beneath another table. It was going to take a lot to shift him, but the whimpering and whining did it in the end.

He opened one bleary eye and with a herculean effort clambered to his feet. The table above him wobbled and tipped over, sending a cascade of knives, forks and spoons, plates and glasses, clattering and crashing onto the patio floor. It nearly ended in a fight, and not between the dogs.

So much for a romantic evening under the stars. Maybe that very bright one was the Dog Star. Closer to hand, the hot dry hills withdrew, dark and mysterious, into the night.

CHILLED OUT

Roberta emerged from the kitchen with a gust of steam and Brussels sprouts. 'Has everybody got a drink?' she called in an attempt to be jolly. 'Adam, what are you drinking?'

'Bacardi and Coke, mum.'

Roberta couldn't help herself. 'Why,' she asked in that oddly hesitant way that got right up some people's noses. 'Why do you always have to be different?'

It was the same every year. Adam crashed his glass down on a table, spilling the contents, and stormed out of the room and out of the house, slamming the front door behind him.

I finished my sherry and made a less spectacular exit. The deepening murk of mid-winter threw into relief other interiors, with fairy lights and Christmas trees and orgies of goodwill.

One brightly lit room was more like a tableau. A large dining table was abandoned to the dirty plates and dishes, nut shells, orange peel, paper streamers and spent crackers. Not quite. Old grandad was fallen forward in his chair with his paper hat on, fast asleep face down in his plum pudding and custard.

Someone in an open neck shirt and hands thrust deep into his trouser pockets for warmth, joined me in contemplation of the scene.

I turned to Adam. 'Says it all, really.'

RED ALERT

Herpes Zoster is not the name of an ancient fire god, it's shingles, but the pain is like being burnt alive.

'Oh, you poor boy!' Rosalind cried. 'You should be home in bed.' I know, but she wasn't there to tuck me in, which is why I brought my copy round to their offices. To see her.

Not for long. The red light flashed by her phone. Toby had first call. Stripped down to those broad scarlet braces dyed in the blood and guts of his minions, he'd bawled and bullied his way up the publishing ladder and didn't know how to stop. Listen to him now.

Rosalind came rushing back out of his office and was straight on the phone, to change the flight to New York for Toby and his wife. The shame and the humiliation. The weekly hotel date with Toby, then to yell at her like that, for everyone to hear and half the street as well.

She finished, looked up and made a big thing of blowing her nose. She tried a brave little smile, smoothing away some of those tell-tale lines of care.

'We're a fine pair, aren't we!' Yes, and why couldn't we have had a go? At least I'd still be there when she woke up.

OLD PAL

Treading water, Debbie and I rose and fell with each little wave before it broke with a sigh upon the shore.

Back on the beach, Miriam sat in her patch of shade, chubby legs red where the sun had briefly touched them. She couldn't swim and anyway she'd be too scared of the sharks and the jellyfish. How different could two sisters be?

At least Miriam had found a friend in Pal. With his long snout and pointed ears, he made me think of the jackal-headed Egyptian god Anubis. But we called him Pal on account of the name on the tins of dog food Miriam bought for him, together with a bowl. He'd filled out nicely in the last few days, and his coat looked much better too.

I came out of the water and Pal sat up and licked his balls. Debbie followed and tripped over him, reaching for her towel. 'Better say goodbye to him now,' she said sharply to her sister. 'There won't be time in the morning.' I'd clean forgotten. We were off again tomorrow.

There was a moment when the temperature dipped before the hot blanket of night came down. The moment to watch Pal settle down on the sand next to his bowl. He'd be waiting in the morning.

I pressed Miriam's hand and whispered, 'He'll be all right.'

NIGHT WATCH

When I climbed the stairs, there were heaps of dead wasps on the floor and a faint smell of death hung in the hot and airless room. Others still buzzed and wandered up and down the window panes, till they'd drop in their turn.

In the silence of the house, a ceaseless rustling and nibbling also reached my ears. It came from above the ceiling, over by the wall. A wasps' nest in the roof.

I'd always quite liked wasps, with their gaily striped bodies, long slender wings, little nodding heads, their taste for honey and jam, and they didn't sting if you left them alone.

A point to reflect upon, as I lay prostrate upon the bed, nauseous and feverish, pulse racing madly, face and hands swollen and the colour of strawberry jam. Trying to shove a piece of paper into the crack in the ceiling, where they were dropping down into the room, wasn't leaving them alone.

I'd loved that house for so many years, filled it with books and paintings, and with the incense of wood smoke, that lingered through each winter and greeted me each spring.

Now I was selling the place, I had betrayed its trust, and it had summoned those wasps to drive me out or kill me first.

I lay wide-eyed in the dark listening to that infernal rustling and nibbling and prayed for the long, long night to end.

Remember this. We don't haunt places. They haunt us.

DINNER DATE

Hoagy Carmichael and The Nearness of You. Nice and slow and not too much of a sweat.

Seated at the baby grand in a corner of the big dining room, doors and windows open to the boom of surf at lunch time, to the oil-calm sea as the blood-red sun went down, I watched her watching me across the floor.

I'd already spotted her down by the pool, lying under a shade, reading a book, quite happy to be left on her own. She was no spring chicken, but she'd kept a figure that said she still had something to give. You can tell.

Now at dinner, one of a jolly party, hair just starting to grey and brushed back over the ears, and in a silvery dress that shimmered as she moved, she chatted and laughed on cue, while her eyes were otherwise engaged.

Her husband, it had to be, losing it on top and gaining it round the middle, dispatched the waiter with a gin and tonic for the pianist. I nodded and smiled my thanks, and she didn't know where to look.

The Nearness of You. With a scraping of chairs, still laughing and chatting, they all got up to go. One last quick glance over her lightly tanned shoulder for us both to remember.

Too bad, we tacitly agreed, that's life.

CURTAIN CALL

Another first night and Tony as Canon Chasuble elbowed his way back to the bar with a painful dig in the ribs for Peter who made an exquisite Algernon. Peter's special friend Jeremy, the director, noticed and took a step forward. He played rugby too.

Julia fiddled with Lady Bracknell's wig and pressed my hand. 'See you round the car park in ten minutes.'

Outside in the cold and sobering night, I wondered about all the bitchiness behind those happy smiling curtain calls. And was it worse among amateurs who felt they'd missed their true vocation and all the more jealously guarded their hopes and dreams?

Coming up the path to the car park a figure in dog collar and gaiters tripped and fell into a puddle. I heard Peter's giggle. Tony picked himself up, fists clenched. Jeremy emerged from the shadows.

Julia tugged at her seat belt. 'Let's go.'

We drove over Hampton Court Bridge and into a cosy world of large half-timbered houses, gentrified pubs, and a church that flew the flag of Saint George.

How did it go? Saint George for England! Saint Pancras for Scotland! A good old chestnut for Tony in the Tudor Players' Christmas pantomime, if he still had his teeth.

LOST LADY

'Excuse me.' She sat on a low garden wall with a shopping bag beside her. The voice was as fragile as the rest of her. 'Do you know the name of this road? You see, I've forgotten where I live.'

It's not every day you meet someone who's just lost a piece of their mind. It was a shock.

I waved a hand about me. 'Do you recognise any of this?'

She shook her head, then raised a thin, blue-veined hand against the sun. 'I say, just behind you, isn't that a beautiful rose!'

The creamy white bloom was tinged with crimson, a floral menstruation, something she wouldn't have to worry about any more.

'Yes,' I agreed, 'and down the road there's a big bush of lavender. I love watching the bees, especially the bumble bees, buzzing and bobbing from flower to flower.'

'I can see,' the old lady said, 'that you haven't lost a sense of wonder. You must be a very happy man.'

I shook my head in turn. 'The more aware you are of everything around you, the more you can get hurt.'

The other smiled sweetly. 'All the same, talking to you has made me feel so much better!'

I smiled back. 'Me too!'

That's the trouble with conversations. You soon forget what started them.

OPEN WIDE

It sounded bad enough from the waiting room, as the dentist dug out Lisa's badly impacted molar, piece by tiny piece. It had taken three stiff vodkas and a handful of sedatives to drag her out of the house, into my car and off to the surgery in the first place.

I recalled Lisa's talents as a children's book illustrator and the great career she had ahead of her till the agoraphobia kicked in and the work dried up.

What was it like just to sit there, day in day out, beneath that faded piece of artwork for Cinderella, terrified to feel the fresh air and the sun upon her face.

The trip to the dentist had been her first day out in years.

Nothing else in that house wanted to leave either, the worn-out mops and brushes in the bath (when did she take one?), the broken chair, busted telly, withered plants, threadbare carpets, the dust and grime that made you cough and sneeze.

'I want a drink,' Lisa mumbled, home again and clutching an antiseptic pad to her butchered jaw.

'You've had enough,' Tom shouted back. He hadn't worked in years. They needed each other to yell at.

'Take care,' he said to me, as I tripped over a bundle of old newspapers in the bare hallway.

NORTHERN LINE

'To the cute little blonde on the 8.31 from Sydenham to Charing Cross. I was the guy in the orange T shirt who couldn't take his eyes off you. Drink?'

I glanced up from the personal ads in the freebie press and we met each other's gaze for perhaps the longest three seconds in both our lives.

We were left in shock, sitting there in the sanitised white light of the compartment, not daring to look again, hardly daring to breathe. Goodge Street, Tottenham Court Road, Leicester Square. If one of us got up to go, what would the other one do?

Embankment, and back into the tunnel, now beneath the river and the stanchions of Hungerford Bridge that carried the cute little blonde and her ogling admirer on the 8.31 into Charing Cross.

Waterloo, and like two puppets on a string we both jumped up. She stood waiting by the doors with her back half to me, and if I'd stretched out a hand and touched her, we'd have blown every fuse from High Barnet to Morden.

Still behind her on the platform, up the steps, along the winding corridor, onto the escalator.

And into history.

BLUE EYES

Mr Smoky was everybody's friend, a coat of grey fur as thick as a Persian rug, and when he saw me coming he rolled over on his back, a sure sign of trust.

Not like Blue Eyes, scampering for cover under the nearest car, or dashing back into that garden of the empty house at the corner of the street.

Jungle was a better name for it, an unchecked riot of vegetation. Peer close enough and you might have come face to face with one of Henri Rousseau's fabulous tigers, unless it was Blue Eyes herself. They were the biggest thing about her, like the eyes of a starving child.

That was before they started clearing the place up. Then where was Blue Eyes? Look no further. Sitting on the front doorstep, cleaning her paws in the welcome sun and waiting for someone to return.

Now it's flowers again in the garden and curtains in the windows. But that's not Blue Eyes dozing on the doorstep. A similar coat but far too well-groomed for her.

Still, she was happy for a week or two, which is as good as it gets for most of us.

PAPER TIGER

Richard could see it in his mind's eye. Tippoo's Tiger on the cover of his book.

This mechanical wonder, digging its claws into a helpless red-coated soldier, had once belonged to the Sultan Tippoo of Mysore, killed in 1799 fighting against the army of the British East India Company. Now on display in the Victoria and Albert museum, Tippoo's Tiger had also inspired Richard to write an account of the Sultan's life and times. He didn't know what he was taking on. I'd watched him go bald and myopic as he laboured at his mammoth task. And he wasn't finished yet. 'I must get out there,' he said. To India.

That left Blow Job, the novel he was going to take to Hollywood, to turn into a movie with a starring role for himself. He must get back into acting.

Up on Richard's wall was an old poster for a production of King Lear, with his name proudly listed among the cast. Someone else in that venerable cast list was now a star of stage and screen. It hadn't happened for him.

He blinked through his glasses and reached for my bottle on the floor where the lino curled up at the edges. 'I mean,' he said, 'what have I got to lose?'

Not his hair, I guess.

TIBBET'S RIDE

Frau Goering, as I called her, had a head the size of a medicine ball, the torso of a tank, and she marched like a juggernaut to a slow-motion goosestep. Above all, she scared me shitless.

On sunny afternoons, I waited for her to pass beneath my window before following at a safe distance, up the Hill as far as the Green Man, where she always turned right, leaving me to continue my stroll by the Heath as far as Tibbet's Corner.

Mr Tibbet, highwayman and footpad, was said to have been hanged on that spot. He never existed so he wasn't, but he fitted the bill, and that's how history is made. A lesson in the hallowing effects of time as well. A thief and a murderer, in fact or fiction, now affectionately remembered by two place names and a monument. There he was, in profile, tricorne hat, frock coat, flintlock in hand, raised high above the circling traffic and daffodils at his feet.

He wouldn't recognise busy Tibbet's Ride today. But I knew the figure crossing the dual-carriageway by the lights and turning in my direction, the brown-belted raincoat, the brogues, and the plod of a fat Reichsmarschall.

They never managed to hang him. Try her, with a strong enough rope.

VIA CRUCIS

'Pity about the mistral,' I shouted. Dark cypresses, grown old and ample on the compost of death, swayed to the roar and whistle of the wind.

I loved that cemetery whatever the weather, but it was the chapel we'd really come to see. As a man of the cloth I thought it might interest David, and Jessica of course. Bags of atmosphere.

The heavy oak door slammed shut behind us and the sudden silence was awesome. A few benches were drawn up before the bare white altar and a faint blue light from one small east window fell like a tear upon the flagstones. We breathed in the smell of cold stone.

Jessica drew her shawl closer about her. 'This place,' she said, 'gives me the creeps.'

Never mind. Back at my place, with a glass of something to see them on their way, it was a chance to show them the large wrought iron crucifix that hung above my fireplace. I'd found it by the cemetery dump, though it must once have marked somebody's grave.

'I sometimes wonder,' I said, 'if their troubled spirit comes round here looking for it.'

Jessica drained her glass. 'David, it's time we made a move.' She stuck her head out of their car window. 'We'll pray for you,' she cried, as the mistral blew them away in a cloud of dust.

CREEPY CRAWLIES

Open Day at the Insect House. 'Of course,' Kate reminded us, 'spiders aren't insects, they're arachnids. But we're all one big happy family in here.'

Big was certainly the word for Judy from Trinidad, with eight hairy legs like fingers dangling from Kate's own hand.

So what was this arachnophobia, this blind horror lodged so deep in our collective unconscious? Hard to say in the case of the tiny money spider and her promise of good luck. The ones you sometimes found in the bath were more like it. Bloated grey bellies suspended between eight long segmented legs and a manic turn of speed. The cocoons they spun in dark corners, waiting motionless, pinhead eyes unblinking, till the moment came to pounce and bite and paralyse and gorge. Spawn of the Devil.

'Don't the females eat their mates?' asked a youth with a bad case of acne.

'Sometimes Derek.' Kate evidently knew him. She stroked Judy's walnut-sized abdomen, as if to say, don't listen to the nasty man.

Back in her glass case, Derek peered closer. With his squint, how many legs could he count? Sixteen? Try him with a millipede.

LAUGHING SAL

The salt-caked windows of Cliff House looked onto a stretch of spume-wet promenade, the hump of Seal Rock and five thousand miles of ocean, all the way to Japan.

Diana turned back to the clutter of pinball tables, baseball games, a miniature crane dangled over a heap of tarnished trinkets and charms. The musty graveyard of a penny arcade.

I dropped a dime into the slot of a small mechanical organ or calliope, fed by wheezy bellows and rubber tubes like dissected veins and arteries. Diana clapped her hands over her ears to the blare of The Stars And Stripes Forever.

Not something Laughing Sal could do. A limbless torso in polka dot red and white smock, she had a shiny face topped by a ginger wig and a grin that promised blue murder.

At the drop of another dime, she began to shudder and shake inside her glass case and to laugh and scream, like someone bawling into a large empty jar. You could be drowning out there, reaching for a grip on the guano-white sides of Seal Rock, the water heaving and sucking you down, while Sal went on laughing and screaming fit to bust.

'Some bloody holiday,' Diana sobbed.

BUNNY CLUB

As soon as she got on the train at Earl's Court I recognised those two front teeth, the way they rested on the lower lip to give her an expression of – how to put it – glum content.

The dating agency had given me her phone number. She didn't sound too bad when I called – though you'd be a fool to put any faith in that – and we arranged to meet by the bookstall at Holborn station. She'd be wearing a lucky rabbit's foot in the lapel of her coat.

Up the escalator, with a half stab of arousal, and there she was, with her lucky rabbit's foot and that look of glum content.

Why waste each other's time. Straight down the other escalator, back onto the platform of the Piccadilly Line, into the train, back into the tunnel, the peristaltic wobble of wires and pipes along the tunnel wall keeping one big lump of shit on the move.

Green Park and Suzie got up to go, catching my eye as she did so. Not a flicker. Of course not, you lousy bastard. Suzie Rose. How long, I wonder, did she wait by the bookstall, all of twenty years ago.

Bye bye Suzie for a second time. Forgive me if you can.

BABY FACE

'Can you take Baby for a walk?' Beth pleaded as she mopped up in the car. She was into pet therapy, but leave Baby alone with anyone for five minutes and they'd be ready to jump off the Brooklyn Bridge.

With a glimpse of the Catskill Mountains across the Hudson river, things might not be so bad when it came to a walk. Besides, I wanted to find out what lay round the corner of leafy Mulberry Street.

A large period residence, upmarket psycho, stood well back from the road across a stretch of lawn and behind a row of trees. Sombre and aloof, it was also empty, sad and loveless.

Stand very still to hear the ghostly chime of the grandfather clock at the foot of the dark mahogany stairs, the creak of a floorboard in the lonely attic room where the piebald rocking horse still tipped gently to and fro.

Someone else had gone very quiet, crouched by the side of the road trying something more ambitious. Baby finished and looked hopefully up at me. We all need love, superannuated, incontinent, grubby off-white poodles most of all.

'Come on, for God's sake.' I tugged at his lead before anyone else saw what we'd done.

DELHI BELLY

'Monsoon?' Geraldine snapped. 'Rubbish!' Okay, but I'd never heard rain like it. A solid roar. I could hardly think to play scrabble. How about otiose? 'That's not a word!' she objected.

Geraldine had invited me to join her on one of her trips buying gems and batiks for her boutique. We'd stay with dear Florrie. We'd have such fun.

She won the scrabble and wanted a drink. With ice, of course. Scotch on the rocks for one.

'Poor wee soul,' Florrie said in the morning as we watched the ambulance depart. 'I'll swear it's nothing I gave you.' Cornflakes, toast and marmalade, a pot of tea.

She lit a new cigarette from the stub of the old, the last gasp of the Raj, and clapped her hands at a fat old crow perched on the window ledge. 'They keep down the cockroaches,' she added. This one took off with a dip of his wing and a bellyful of cockroach.

The aircraft dipped a silver wing over the fuzz of lights below. Lying in the dark down there, listening to the hum and whirr of the fan and waiting for the next faint gust of air, till someone got up from their bed rather fast and started making dreadful noises in the bathroom.

'Drink sir?' They were soon round with the trolley. 'Ice?'
'No thanks.'

EN VACANCES

Swifts and swallows wheeled and dived, catching the sunlight on their wings and translating it into little shrieks of joy. We drove through Pont Saint Esprit. Bridge of the Holy Spirit.

Dora clapped her hands. 'Isn't that a lovely name, dear!' Reg swiped at a fly.

Auntie Dora and Uncle Reg, who used to send me socks for Christmas. I'd almost forgotten them till they turned up on my doorstep with a few hours to spare from their coach tour. I'd take them somewhere, better than sitting on my terrace trying to think of things to say.

We parked among the parasol pines and Reg spoke at last. He pointed to another car. 'Dutch,' he sniffed.

'Take your cap off, dear,' Dora gently chided him, as we stepped into the dim cool interior of the Abbey, with painted columns rising to a vaulted ceiling of midnight blue patterned with stars.

She reached for my hand. 'It's so lovely to see you again after all these years. Reg doesn't say much, but I know he's loving it too.' She added in a whisper and with a shy little smile, 'D doesn't really stand for Dutch, does it?'

Back in the car, hands on knobbly knees, nose starting to peel, Reg blurted, 'Think I don't know what D really stands for?'

Dora reached for her tissues. Reg swiped at a fly. 'Bloody Jerries!'

BLUE NOTE

'All right,' Henry replied softly and as always to Harriet's request, 'if you twist my arm.' I'd like to see her try, or anybody else. Henry was built like a heavyweight, though he didn't play Rachmaninov with the gloves on.

He now dabbed politely at his mouth with his napkin, got up from the dinner table and padded obediently across the Persian rug to Harriet's waiting baby grand. Brahms this time, the notes falling from his fingers like autumn raindrops, while Harriet served coffee and passed round the chocolate mints.

'Great stuff Henry!' I cried at the end, perhaps a little high on the sherry trifle. 'Now how about some Blues?' After one of his occasional town hall recitals I'd joined him at the keyboard and we'd had great fun with Charlie Davenport's Cow Cow Boogie till the caretaker chucked us out.

Henry's eyes lit up beneath his bushy brows. They met Harriet's stony gaze. 'Thank you Henry. We mustn't let you miss your train.'

I drove him back to the station. 'Any more recitals coming up?' Apparently not. His agent had dropped him. A scholarship and three years at the Royal College of Music were not enough.

Even for a chocolate mint.

FAG END

There's a line in some play about seeing the skull behind the skin. Whoever wrote it must have been thinking of Cyril. He was a head hunter's trophy, the grey shrunken toothy grin, the random tufts of hair. If that's what forty fags a day for forty years had done, they'd also kippered and cured him of all infection. He never missed a party. He was as indestructible as a flea, and just as tenacious, if he got hold of you. Take evasive action fast.

'Hi there!' I tucked myself in next to Anthea over by the door. Her face was no oil painting, but the rest of her I fancied something rotten. 'Good party!'

Toying with his next cigarette, Cyril bobbed up between us. 'I just wanted to ask you,' he began in his gas pipe voice. I looked round for moral support. Anthea had gone. So had I.

Outside in the bleak courtyard I could at least breathe again. Round the corner I jumped on a bus. Cyril hopped on behind me. He flashed his freedom pass, sat down by my side with his dandruff, and fiddled with his hearing aid. 'How far are you going?'

All the way with Anthea, given half a bleedin' chance.

COMMAND PERFORMANCE

Bob and Sam, man and dog, squatted on the pavement outside the bank, strategically placed for a hand-out. I dropped a few more coins into their cap and Sam rolled his big brown eyes and nuzzled his cold wet nose into my hand.

It was no life for a dog his size, consigned all day beneath that filthy old blanket, looking doleful. All the same, he looked in better shape than his master. Bob's face was pinched and ashen, and his grin was not a pretty sight.

It hadn't improved any in the picture of him in the local newspaper, above a story that proved how deceptive appearances can be. It seemed that he'd been living for years on benefits in a smart council house and with a small fortune stashed away.

You could say he'd earned it, hunched on the pavement under that blanket, come rain come shine, chewing on a bun washed down with the dregs of cold tea in a plastic cup, though the prospect of champagne and caviar for supper may have helped him endure it.

A menu somewhere in between, I'd say, while he was detained at Her Majesty's pleasure, though I couldn't speak for poor old Sam.

SMOKE SIGNALS

That boulder had to be a meteorite, shiny black and of an unimaginable weight. God knows how it got there, but it stood at the corner of the Rue de l'Horloge, where my neighbour, face like a wrinkled walnut, woolly stockings and clogs, sat on fine summer days and watched the world go by.

She lived by the sun. The squeak and groan of her wooden shutters as she opened them on their rusty hinges told me that the sun was up. The squeak and groan as she closed them again told me that the sun had set.

The smoke from her chimney was less predictable. It emerged at odd times as a yellowish cloud and carried with it the stench of smouldering scraps of bone and gristle, rotten vegetables, or worse. 'Ordures' was the word.

I might have complained to the Mairie, but returning one springtime, I didn't need to. As impossible as it seemed, the shutters squeaked and groaned, the chimney smoked no more, the boulder was an empty throne.

I visited the cemetery to pay my respects. I looked for her grave in vain. But watching from my terrace as the swifts and swallows wheeled and screamed in the radiant evening light, my eyes were drawn back to that chimney. How black it appeared against the sky.

Spontaneous combustion. What else.

STILL LIFE

Carol had had a rotten time, what with a messy divorce and a wayward young daughter to bring up, and this was her first real holiday in years. She yawned extravagantly, the flush of last night's wine still on her face. 'I dreamed of those sparrows,' she said, as we breezed along in the car, forever chasing the same distant grey-blue line of hills.

She spoke of the ones we'd seen in the famous abbey at Vezelay, flitting and chirping about the nave. We didn't expect to find birds inside a church in our squeaky clean age, though what could be more natural, God's creatures in God's house, the commonplace and the numinous made one.

Like those pilgrims who gathered there a thousand years ago, a noisy scruffy crowd, suddenly transfigured by the clamour of the bells high above their heads, the wide-eyed stone image of Christ at the entrance to that majestic nave.

'We've lost our sense of wonder,' I said, just as the hills finally parted to reveal our first vineyard, the neatly staked out rows of vines, young shoots aflame, calling down the sun.

We turned a corner and spread across the road was the freshly mangled body of a fox or a hare.

'Oh God.' Carol buried her face in her hands. Sometimes you just can't win.

COPY CAT

'That's new,' I said of Van Gogh's Sunflowers, propped against The Fighting Temeraire, which was propped against The Hay Wain, which was propped against the television.

Oliver spent his retirement making life-size copies of old masters, in a council flat that could best be described as cosy. You were greeted by a smiling Mona Lisa at the front door, and in the bathroom you took a piss with The Laughing Cavalier.

'Yes.' Marooned in his armchair, Oliver looked pleased. 'Took a lot of paint, that one. All that impasto.' He twisted his thumb about, as though applying his paints to the canvas. 'The Fauves owed a hell of a lot to Van Gogh. Matisse, Braque, Vlaminck. That crowd.'

'The Wild Beasts.' Pam entered the room sideways, juggling with three plates of sausage and mash. 'That's what *fauves* means in French.'

Not how I'd describe Picasso, a neutered black tom of stupendous girth, who slept among the canvases, the tubes of paint, the jars and brushes in the bedroom.

'Watch that bloody cat!' Oliver spluttered through a mouthful of mashed potato. 'The paint's still wet!'

I slipped Picasso a piece of sausage and watched him expand some more. 'What's next?' I asked Oliver. 'Guernica?'

I winked at Picasso. He blinked at me.

FISH FACE

Lotte crept up behind me. 'Come,' she whispered in my ear. 'I need you.'

For her birthday party she'd bought a large fresh fish that presently flopped over the kitchen sink, a bit too big to go in the oven. She handed me her sharpest knife. 'Please to cut off the head.'

The dull white eye of that poor fish stared back at me, the drooping mouth had all the pathos of a clown. I gripped the knife. Which end did it matter, anyhow?

Lotte turned round from peeling potatoes. 'Mein Gott, not the bloody tail!' She snatched the knife from me and took two or three frantic swipes to sever head from body. Public executions must often have been like that. Hands shaking from her exertions, she added, 'You are just a bloody wimp!'

Without another word I slammed her front door behind me, raced across the road and into my car, catching my own face in the driving mirror. It was just as twisted down one side as Lotte's. Lopsided jobs the lot of us, a good side and a bad.

Across the street a baleful light shone behind Lotte's curtains. Some birthday party. Run back now, said Dr Jekyll, kiss and make up before it's too late. With a crunch of gears, Mr Hyde tore off down the road.

HAPPY DAYS

'What a game, eh!' With a white carnation in his buttonhole and a bottle of bubbly in his hand, he joined me on the bench and held out the bottle. 'Like some?'

'Thanks.' I took a swig and wiped the neck of the bottle. 'Not your wedding, is it?'

'Not this time!' he chuckled, just a shade uncomfortably I thought, as we watched the rest of them gather outside the big gothic house in the park to have their pictures taken. 'You been married?'

'Divorced.' You can sometimes speak more freely with a stranger than with a friend. 'That was the easy part. It's love affairs that really kill you off.' I took another swig. 'You can't win.'

'Terry!' A young woman wearing a floral hat and gripping a large shiny black handbag, stood a little way down the path. 'Where've you been?' She beckoned impatiently, with a sour look at me. 'Come on. It's going to pour in a minute.'

The sky had turned the colour of a deep and wounding bruise, and with a flicker and a rumble there came that rare and passing fragrance as the first swollen raindrops soaked into warm dry ground.

Terry straightened his collar and tie, clambered to his feet, crushed out his cigarette. 'What a game, eh!'

WEATHER REPORT

'I've got so many things wrong with me I dunno' where to start.' Danny used to cross the road to avoid me. Not anymore. 'Haemorrhoids. They're drivin' me mental.'

Did they have anything to do with the fact that the crutch on those old jeans reached almost down to his knees? At least his wedding tackle, should he ever have need of it, had all the world to swing in.

'You're right.' Danny's mind spun like a catherine wheel and his words came out with a flash and a splutter. 'I should get a job. That's it. Otherwise I'm just bloody useless.'

With his strabismus I never knew which eye was fixed on me or which one I should focus on. 'It's the weather. Christmas? What a joke. Makes you want to top yourself.'

A thin drizzle settled on his thick unruly locks and clung to the ends of his drooping Pancho Villa moustache. My packet of cornflakes was getting wet too. But if it helped him to talk. A spot of therapy.

Danny hitched up his jeans to no visible effect. 'You're right. It's all in the mind. Still, you gotta laugh!' Through the gap in those tombstones that served as his two front teeth.

WATER SPORTS

The chorus of crickets and cicadas almost drowned out Millicent's little scream. She'd disturbed a tarantula spider under a piece of wood, the genuine article, native to the Midi, not some tropical monster, though still a healthy size. 'Kill it!' she gasped.

'Just leave it alone.' Always something with Millicent. She was the one who wanted to work up a tan. Well, here we were, among the crumbling stone terraces, the parched clumps of lavender and withered rows of vines, the dead and dying almond trees, all cracked and twisted under the weight of heat.

The ruined farmsteads said it all. The heaps of rock and stone, the fallen rafters and broken tiles. Abandoned long ago.

But wait. A few steps away from one of them, a pair of wooden shutters set into the hillside opened upon a large stone cistern of crystal clear water. What a place to sport in on such a day, like some joyful mythic nymph. Just don't let those shutters close on you again. Nothing to cling onto, no one to hear you, no one to know, up there in the lonely sun-baked hills.

Crouching in a patch of shade, her face now a lobster red, Millicent kicked at the empty water bottle.

I smiled and beckoned. 'Come over here and take a dip.'

LAST WALTZ

'That's the way to pull the birds,' said Walter, fondly fingering the keys on his old alto sax.

It probably was, up there on stage behind his monogrammed music desk while the glitter ball flashed about the dance floor and he eyed them up while their partner's back was turned.

He hadn't got so much hair these days for the Brylcreem to shine on, but just the two of us were going to do it all over again at the Playmates Club Christmas dance.

'Good evening, Ladies and Gentlemen,' Walter bawled into the microphone to a shriek of feedback. 'Let's Face the Music and Dance!' Not while there was a sausage roll or a mince pie remaining from the buffet. Then came the raffle.

The brutal thump of the club ghetto blaster pursued us in the rain from the church hall back to my car. The tambourine Walter had bought to double on, when things got really hot, was never out of its case.

He snatched off his soggy pink paper hat. 'If that's what they want,' he blubbered, 'they can all get fucking stuffed!'

Birds or boilers, Gladys, Hermione, Olive, stuffed or otherwise.

SEA FEVER

On Ocean Beach fugitive rainbows danced among the tumbling surf, legions of tiny birds ran comically up and down the gleaming wet apron of the sea with each advancing and retreating wave, and the world was as bright and pristine as on the day of creation, save for one small group of kids gathered round something on the sand.

The downward slit of the mouth, the big tail fin curved like a cutlass, they were poking and shoving at a stranded young shark.

Amazing creatures, I told them. Sharks had no real bones, just cartilage and muscle to give them more strength for less weight, skin instead of scales for extra speed through the water, and with those fins they could turn on a dime.

So saying, I stepped boldly forward, picked up the shark in both hands, waded into the sea unmindful of my trousers, and hurled him as far as I could back into the waves.

My good turn for the day, as long as it lasted. Returning on my walk, trousers beginning to dry, he was back on the shore, too weak or too sick to swim against the tide. Voracious predator he might have grown up to be, right now he was a fellow creature in extremis.

And the light went out of the day.

LAST RITES

It must have been at the roundabout outside the cemetery gates that we got stuck in that funeral procession and were driven back, bumper to bumper, to what must be the home of the deceased in the Rue Pasteur.

'Come on,' I said to Jill, as we sat in our little car and watched them disappear inside. 'I reckon they owe us one.' I reached for jacket and tie and ran a comb through my hair. 'Besides, with that crowd they'll never notice us.'

A maid greeted us with drinks on a silver tray. Cognac, Armagnac, it hit the spot.

'They should do a Michelin Guide to some of the cemeteries they have over here,' I said. 'All that masonry, all those cypresses, like candles for a black mass. Crosses for interest, skulls for atmosphere.'

There were tables laden with food and wine. 'The funeral baked meats did coldly furnish forth the marriage table.' I smacked my lips. 'Hamlet.'

'Alas poor Yorick.' Jill waved her glass. 'Like one of your skulls.'

'Keep your voice down.' I handed her a plate and fork. 'Better eat something.'

'A funeral baked bean?' She collapsed with laughter onto a trestle table and slid to the floor with a bowl of mayonnaise.

'I think,' she said next, 'I'm going to be sick.'

LITTLE OTTO

'*I do wish* you wouldn't call me that!' Elizabeth protested as we drove past fields of sugar cane, cows munching at their fringes with a bovine indifference to heat.

'Sorry darling,' Sylvia replied absently and winked at me in the driving mirror.

Back on the beach Elizabeth drove her sunshade into the sand while Sylvia and I stripped down for a swim. At the line of buoys marking the limit of safe bathing she handed me her mask and snorkel, bobbed under the surface of the water, blew a stream of it in my face, winked again and headed back for the shore.

Through the mask I watched something glide effortlessly over the sun-flecked rocks. It was a baby octopus. He found a tiny crevice and tucked himself in till you wouldn't know he was there.

That's what you could do without any bones. Elizabeth's trouble was too many bones. 'How disgusting,' she was shouting as I raised my head from Little Otto's world back to my own. 'Spitting water like that!'

'Bessie darling,' Sylvia pleaded, 'it was just a bit of fun.'

'Fun!' Elizabeth choked on the word and tried running up the sand in her flip flops. 'And I *do wish* you wouldn't call me that!'

CELTIC FRINGE

'Shame about the parade,' I said. The blurred wet city skyline was dotted with those old roof-top water tanks, that looked like grubby urban beehives. Saint Patrick's Day in the rain.

'Ah!' Eamon, our janitor, who lived on top of the block, was shoehorned into a battered armchair that must have collapsed had there been a spare inch of space. 'But they're not what they were in my day.'

We took a drop of the hard stuff in our coffee and I pointed to a picture on the wall. 'That looks like the Giant's Causeway.'

'Ah!' Eamon shifted perilously in his armchair. 'They say 'twas built by the mighty hero Finn MacCool to take himself across the sea to Scotland, at least as far as Fingal's Cave that still bears his name.'

Eamon lit a joint, filling the room with something akin to the smell of peat smoke. 'That was back in the days of the Fianna, the ancient company of knights who gathered by the sacred Hill of Tara in times of trouble.'

We took another drop of the hard stuff. 'All this mind, was long before Saint Patrick.'

Going back down those stairs seemed a lot trickier than going up them. Beth was waiting by the broken elevator, the gate jammed wide open.

'When can he fix it?' she asked.

MEMORY LANE

Memory is fickle. After so long a time I couldn't be sure I'd returned to the right spot in the park or to the same park bench.

The one we'd sat on, not next to each other but at opposite ends, with an ocean of space between us, her face now as cold and expressionless as marble and terrible to behold.

We were finished. We had nothing more to say. So why had I pleaded to see her one more time? Because I couldn't bear to let her go. And that, as the Buddha had said, was the cause of so much distress, not being able to give things up, to let them go.

Forty years on should surely be long enough. Too long perhaps. Memory may be fickle. It also has a nasty habit of catching up with you. The further away events are in time, the closer they crowd in.

'D'you mind?' An attractive woman, slim, well-groomed, mature, stood a few paces off and indicated the place beside me on the bench. She sat down, smiled and waved a hand. 'I love this view.'

I hadn't noticed. I smiled back. 'All yours,' I said, got up and walked away.

FRENCH KISS

You'd be wrong if you thought Gordon was a miserly Scotsman. Those stacks of coins in his gloomy old house behind the Place du Chateau were the change from his shopping that he didn't know what to do with. He couldn't handle the currency. He couldn't speak the language. Whatever had induced him to move abroad and to our village in the first place?

I could never get a straight answer to that one. 'The girl in the boulangerie is quite nice,' he muttered as I tried one more time.

'Funnily enough,' I replied, 'she was asking about you the other day.'

Gordon turned an incandescent red beneath his Caledonian whiskers. He swilled the wine round his glass. He put it to his nose. 'I fear,' he stuttered in his confusion, 'it is still a little t-too young.'

Speaking of age, girl was pushing it. She'd been around, and maybe handling those baguettes, still warm from the oven, turned her on. What did it for me was the way she said 'au revoir', catching at her breath and tickling her epiglottis with the back of her tongue. She could tickle mine any time.

'Shall I give her your love?' I asked Gordon.

We won't see him in the boulangerie again. I'll buy his baguettes for him. Get rid of some of those coins.

POST SCRIPT

If you're in a hole stop digging. I went on compulsively scribbling a word in here, scratching one out there, getting nowhere.

A lousy day all round. Early spring sun and warmth had brought out the blossom and the buds, before it turned cold and wet again. The same thing every year, but they never learned. Outside my window the still tender and unsullied leaves on the trees shivered in the wind.

I felt sorry for them. I felt sorry for that abandoned car down the road with a stack of rain-soaked parking tickets shoved under the windscreen wipers. I felt more sorry for the small fluffy striped tiger left on top of the dashboard, little button eyes raised helplessly to the windscreen and those soggy parking tickets.

The bottom line was that I couldn't walk past that vehicle and its solitary occupant again. Every day I must take the long way round to the shops.

Why did I feel such pity for inanimate objects, from cars to fluffy toys? Maybe I should start digging and try to make something out of that.

First things first. With a huge effort I stood up, cold and stiff. Down to the shops, the long way round. Bread, soup, fish fingers.

The author

Alan Blackwood is the author of numerous books and features on music, including a biography of the famous British conductor, Sir Thomas Beecham. More recently he has turned his skills to writing fiction. Many of his very short stories (or flash fiction) have already appeared in print. He is also completing his first novel.

The artist

Seattle-based artist Clare Johnson, who has provided the illustration for the cover of this book, studied art in the United States and in Europe. Her work, striking both to the eye and to the imagination, has made her a major new talent in the world of art and design.

novum ♥ PUBLISHER FOR NEW AUTHORS

The publisher

> **Whoever stops getting better, will in time stop being good.**

This is the motto of novum publishing, and our focus is on finding new manuscripts, publishing them and offering long-term support to the authors.
Our publishing house was founded in 1997, and since then it has become THE expert for new authors and has won numerous awards.

Our editorial team will peruse each manuscript within a few weeks free of charge and without obligation.

You will find more information about
novum publishing and our books on the internet:

www.novum-publishing.co.uk